Puffin Books

Puppets created by Ivor Wood

by Elisabeth Beresford

The Wombles
Make a Clean Sweep

Original film puppets created by Ivor Wood
© FilmFair Ltd, 1972

Photographs by Barry Leith

This is the home of the Wombles who live under
Wimbledon Common. The Wombles are the tidiest
creatures in the world and they spend a great deal of
their time clearing up all the rubbish which people
leave lying about.

One day, on his way to start tidying up, Orinoco,
who is the fattest and laziest Womble, came out of the
burrow holding his nose in a very *peculiar* way.

Wellington, who is rather shy and absent-minded, and who was just coming back from tidying up, said 'Hallo, Orinoco, why are you holding your nose in that *peculiar* way?'

'Because there's a horrible smell in the burrow, that's
why,' said Orinoco. 'A horrible smell that's coming
from the kitchen. It's put me right off my food. Ugh!'
And Orinoco actually hurried away to start work,
which was *most* unusual for him.

Inside the burrow, Great Uncle Bulgaria, who is the oldest and wisest of the Wombles, Tomsk, who is the strongest, and Bungo, who is the bossiest, were all standing outside the kitchen trying *not* to sniff the bad

smells. 'Don't worry, young Wombles,' said Great Uncle
Bulgaria, 'I'm quite sure that Tobermory will soon find
out what's gone wrong in the kitchen, and then he'll put
it right. Meanwhile I think I shall go back to my study.'

Tobermory is the Womble who is in charge of the workshop.

'Can you make the nasty smell go away from my kitchen?' asked Madame Cholet, the cook.

'Yes, I *think* so,' said Tobermory. 'It looks to me as if the chimney above the stove is blocked up, but we'll soon get it cleared. Tomsk, go and get me a brush from the workshop!'

'And as for you, Bungo – off you go to the Common and see if you can clean out the kitchen chimney from *that* end,' ordered Tobermory. 'And hurry up, or we won't get any supper!'

But Bungo didn't know where the kitchen chimney
was on the Common. He couldn't see it anywhere.

Down below the other Wombles were all helping
Tomsk in his efforts to try and clear the chimney.

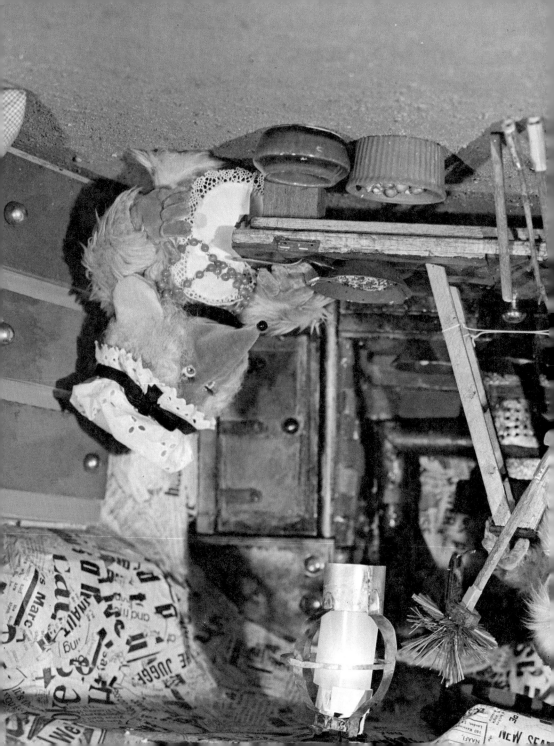

'That's funny,' said Bungo. 'There's a strange noise coming from that old tree stump. Perhaps there's a bird's nest inside it. I'd better have a look to make sure everything is all right . . .'

'Now then, Tomsk,' said Tobermory, 'when I say
"three" I want you to push that brush up the chimney
as hard as you can. Are you ready? One-two-THREE!'

'That's cleared it,' said Tobermory, 'it must have been blocked by an old nest. I'll take up some wire netting to cover the top of the chimney, so that it doesn't happen again.'

'Well done, Tomsk!' said Madame Cholet. 'The nasty smell is all gone. Now I can start cooking the supper.'

'I don't think that was funny at all!' said Bungo crossly,
'pushing old bird's nests in my face like that. Well I'll
show them!' And he pulled with all his strength. . .

... And up went Tomsk.

'That's a good Womble.' said Tobermory, 'you *have* been working hard at clearing the chimney. Now you can help me put some netting over the top of it.

Tck, tck, tck, what's that I wonder?' For at that moment
there was a loud crashing, bashing, roaring noise
under their feet.

The crashing and the bashing and the roaring were all caused by poor Tomsk falling all the way from the

ceiling and knocking over everything. *What* a mess,
and *what* a noise!

'Get out of my way,' said Madame Cholet, 'now I have to sweep up EVERYTHING before I can start cooking. Shoo-shoo-shoo!' Wellington and Tomsk were only too glad to do as they were told.

'Tck, tck, tck,' said Tobermory, 'the kitchen looks in a
bit of a state. What do you think can have happened?'

But Bungo didn't say anything at all. He thought it
might be wiser *not* to know best for once.
Now there'll be no more trouble with bird's nests
blocking up the Wombles' kitchen chimney. 'Mmmm,'
said Bungo, sniffing deeply. 'Something smells good. . .'

Great Uncle Bulgaria, who had been having a nice quiet read in his study, put down his newspaper and sniffed.

'Mmmm,' he said, 'it must be supper time at last. I wonder what we're having? Whatever it is, it smells *very* nice.'

The kitchen is all clean and tidy again and filled with a delicious smell. It is one minute to supper time, but somebody is missing . . .

It's Orinoco, who'd been having forty winks after he'd finished work. 'Mmmm,' he said, 'that horrible smell has all gone and now there is a delicious scent in its place. Why, I do believe I feel quite hungry *after* all! I wonder if anything exciting has happened while I've been out working . . ?' And Orinoco hurried into the burrow as fast as he could.